Two Frogs
in
Trouble

Copyright © 1997 Self-Realization Fellowship

First edition, 1997. This printing, 2012.

We wish to express grateful appreciation for the work of writer Natalie Hale, artist Susie Richards, and computer graphic artist Bentley Richards in the preparation of this book.

ISBN-13: 978-0-87612-351-5
ISBN-10: 0-87612-351-5
Printed in the United States of America on acid-free paper
1679-J2358

Two Frogs in Trouble

Based on a Fable Told
by

Paramahansa Yogananda

Self-Realization Fellowship
FOUNDED 1920
Paramahansa Yogananda

Big Frog snoozed near the pond as the sun warmed the large hump of his back. "What a great day for doing nothing," he thought. But Little Frog bounced in and out of the sunshine as he hopped from toadstool to pond and back again. It was morning at the farm, and Little Frog was ready for fun.

"Wake up! Wake up!" he called to Big Frog. "It's time to play."

Plip! Plip! Plip! Little Frog took off for the pond.

Big Frog's eyes were wide open now. Plop! Plop! Plop! He followed Little Frog, and together they crossed the pond into the barnyard, playing leapfrog and hide-and-seek along the way.

They were having such fun that they forgot it was milking time at the barn.

Plop! Plip! They jumped straight into a pail of fresh milk.

The sides of the pail were slippery, and the frogs couldn't get out. "Help! Help!" yelled Big Frog.

But it was no use. No one came.

Hoping somehow to escape, the two frogs paddled in circles around the milk pail.

They swam for hours.

Big Frog began to swim slower and slower. Finally he groaned, "Why should we keep trying? We will die in this pail. I'm so tired, I can't swim any longer."

"Keep on! Keep on!" cheered Little Frog as he splashed around the pail. "You must have courage, or you will drown. Don't give up!" And so they went on together for a while.

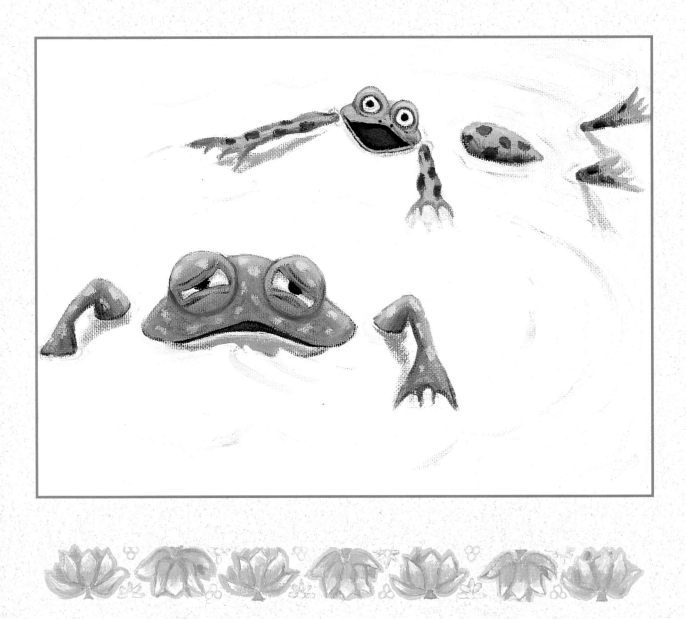

But soon Big Frog stopped swimming. "Little friend," he gasped, "it's no use. We can't get out. I'm going to quit trying."

And so he did.

Now only Little Frog was left. He said to himself, "Well, if I give up, I'll be dead. So I will keep on swimming!"

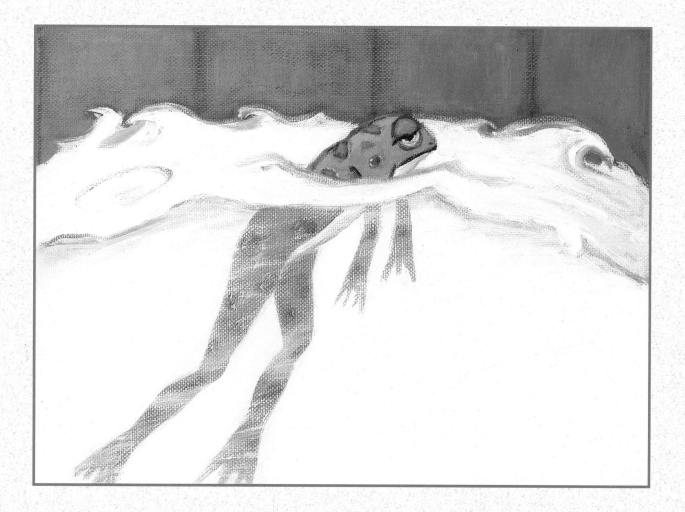

Two more hours passed, and Little Frog's legs could hardly move. "I can't swim another stroke," he moaned. But then he thought of what happened to Big Frog.

With every speck of strength in him, Little Frog cried out, "Even if I die trying, I won't give up."

"While there is life, there's hope!"

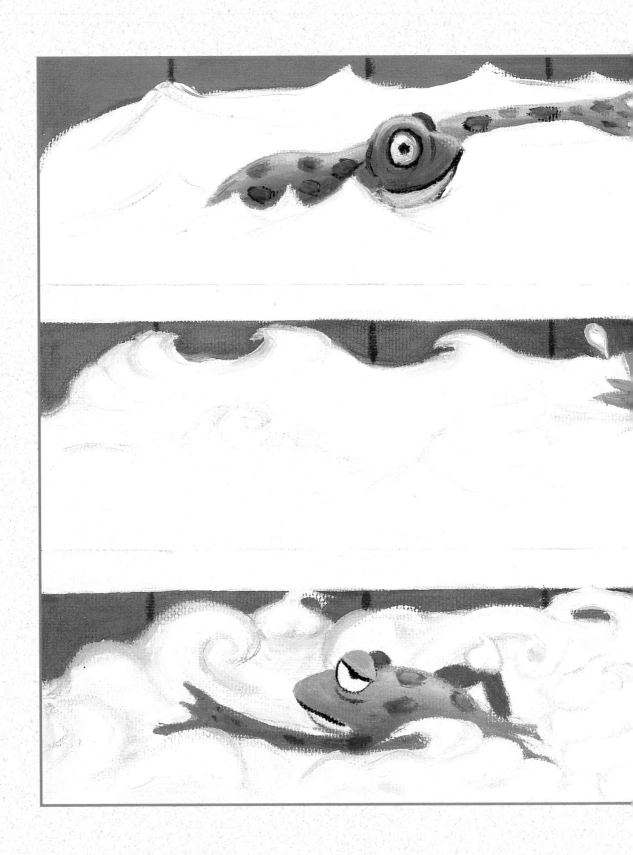

Bursting with courage, Little Frog felt tingling new life and energy come into his legs. He raced around and around the milk pail.

"Splash! Splash! Splash!" For a long time, that was the only sound he heard. But then he began to hear a new sound. "Glop! Glop! Glop!" The white waves had turned to the thickest cream. Now it was even harder to swim, but Little Frog kept on with all his might.

Suddenly, he felt something under him. He looked down and saw his feet resting on a small hill. His swimming had churned the milk to butter! With a great leap of joy, Little Frog jumped out of the pail...

to freedom!

That night, as he hopped happily through the tall grass, Little Frog smiled up at the moon and thought, "Now I know it's true! There is always hope."

"From now on, I will never, ever give up."

And he never did.

Paramahansa Yogananda
(1893–1952)

More than a hundred years ago in India, there lived a boy named Mukunda. There was something very special about Mukunda. Even as a young child, his great love for God and people deeply touched his family and friends.

Soon after he finished high school, he met a wise man who showed him how he could give his whole life to loving God and helping people.

After going to college, Mukunda became a monk like his teacher and was given a new name: Yogananda. He started a "how-to-live" school for children. In addition to the usual subjects, he taught the children how to live a good and happy life, and he often told them stories like the one in this book.

A few years later, Yogananda traveled to America to teach others what he had learned in India. He wrote many books filled with his wonderful wisdom, including his well-known *Autobiography of a Yogi*. Today he is known all over the world as a great spiritual teacher.